T0128631

JAKE and JIL-A-MA-JOO'S ADVENTURE

By Melina and Debra Sylvestro

Illustrated by Gail Jacalan

To order additional copies of this book, contact:
Xlibris
844-714-8691
www.Xlibris.com
Orders@Xlibris.com

ISBN: Softcover   978-1-6698-0094-1
         EBook   978-1-6698-0093-4
         Hardcover   978-1-6698-0127-6

Print information available on the last page

Rev. date: 12/07/2021

JAKE and JIL-A-MA-JOO'S ADVENTURE

In Honor of the Author, Our Beloved
Mother, Nana, Sister, Friend
Melina Sylvestro
1932 – 2020

Melina was born and raised in Lyndhurst, NJ, the daughter of Italian immigrants. She was 1 of 10 children, including her twin sister Josephine and twin brothers, Bob and Frank. Melina was a strong and generous woman of faith. She had a creative flair and a passion for life. She became a single mother in the early 1960's and raised 3 children, Debra, Michael and Robert. In both good and challenging times, mom kept a positive attitude and always "found a way" to learn, grow and make life better for her family and everyone in her life. Her beautiful smile 'lit up the room" and she had a great sense of humor.

Melina loved to be around children and they were drawn to her warm, nurturing spirit and sense of fun. She created this story, Jake and Jil-a-ma-joo's Adventure and repeatedly told it to her youngest son Robert, in the late 1960's. Many years later she wrote it down from memory, while taking a children's writing class. Several other stories followed, yet this one was her favorite and her goal was to have it published and share it with many other children and families.

Melina believed that each child is a special gift and deserves to be treated with love and respect.

All things are possible with God. Keep the Faith and Follow your Dreams!

Twin Siblings Josephine [l] Melina [r] and Bob,Frank [center]

Melina,Debra,Robert [l], Michael [r]

Mom- We are eternally grateful for your unconditional love and devotion. You were an amazing mother and we are so proud of you!

Acknowledgment

Our heartfelt thanks to the many family members and friends who were a part of Melina's life. Your love and support meant the world to her and to our family. Love Always- Debra, Mike and his wife Neva, Robert and his wife Jayne.

Melina deeply loved and cherished her 5 grandchildren and her beautiful legacy will continue to live on throughout their lives. Her grandchildren describe their "nana" with these qualities:

Robbie-   Strong, Resilient, Independent, Resourceful, Disciplinarian, Travel Enthusiast
Ariana-   So Loving and Caring, Determined, Strong-willed
Corey-   Loyal, Devoted, Nurturing, Loving
Michael-   Resilient, Loving and Kind
Nick-   Inspirational, Nurturing ,Encouraging

Nana, Robbie and Ariana   Nana and Corey   Nana and Michael   Nana and Nick

Robbie, Ariana, Michael, Nick, Corey

This story begins on a sunny, bright, beautiful day in Jake's backyard. Jake is having fun playing with Jil-a-ma-joo; his dog and his best friend. He always has lots of fun with Jil-a-ma-joo teaching him tricks, running with him in the park and throwing him the Frisbee.

The screen door is opened and Jake's Mom is in the kitchen starting to cook dinner. She hollers out to him, "Jake, oh Jake, I need you to go to the store to buy bread for dinner tonight." "O.K. Mom," Jake hollers back. "I'll take Jil-a-ma-joo with me." "That will be fine," she says, "but be very careful and be sure to take his leash and don't be too long."

They start to walk down the street and Jake begins to skip and sing happily while Jil-a-ma-joo is stopping at every tree to sniff and kick up some dirt. "Let's go Jilly," Jake said. "We've got to be moving along and get to the store."

Duck Pond
Lane

2

Sometimes Jake would take off Jil-a-ma-joo's leash and the dog would grab it from him and carry it between his teeth. Everyone would smile and laugh when they saw him. It was a funny sight to see indeed! Jake decides to go another way and they walk down this street with beautiful trees and houses called "Duck Pond Lane."

As they are walking along the path of grass alongside the curb, suddenly Jake sees this shining article on the ground that shines in his eyes. When the sun hit it, it really sparkled! Jilly, (as Jake liked to call him sometimes), started to sniff and bark at it. Jake bent over and picked it up. His blue eyes popped wide open. "WOW!", he said. "This is totally awesome."

Duck Pond
Lane

4

Sitting in the palm of his hand was a gorgeous diamond bracelet. It certainly looked like diamonds anyway! "Holy Maloney! I can't believe this," Jake said. "What should I do?" Jake turned to Jil-a-ma-joo and said, "What are we going to do? We can't keep this. It is worth a lot of money. Anyway, that would not be very honest. Tell you what Jilly, I will hold this bracelet very carefully and we'll go home and tell Mom. She will know what to do. What do you say?" Jilly bent his head to the side and looked up at Jake, with a silly look on his face. "I knew you would agree. Let's go home!"

They are walking home, when a little down the road Jake sees this tall woman sobbing and shaking her head from side to side. She looked very pretty and was standing by a big, beautiful Weeping Willow Tree. The branches were different shades of green, hanging all around her. She was leaning against the big, brown tree trunk, when Jake walked over to her and said, "What's wrong? Are you O.K? Why are you crying?" The woman picked up her head, still sobbing and said, "Oh my, I am so very, very sad and so very upset. Something awful has happened."

"My husband gave me such a lovely gift for our Wedding Anniversary and now I've lost it and I don't know what I am going to tell him," she said, still sobbing. "Ma'am, is this what you are looking for?", Jake said, taking the beautiful bracelet very carefully out of his pocket. "Oh, yes! Yes! That is my lovely bracelet." She was jumping up and down with joy. "Oh. Thank you! Thank you so much." She hugged and kissed Jake. "You have made me so happy." She leaned over and gave Jil-a-ma-joo a great big hug, too.

"By George, you have made me the happiest lady in the whole world. I am going to give you a wonderful reward for being such an honest boy. I am going to call your mom on the telephone and tell her how very proud I am of you."

"My name is Mrs. Ellen Greenstreet. And what may I ask is your name, young man, and your wonderful dog's name?" "My name is Jake," he said, "and this is my dog, Jil-a-ma-joo, Jilly for short. He is my best friend." "I could see that", said Mrs. Greenstreet. "Let's go across the street and you can meet Mr. Greenstreet and we can tell him the whole exciting story about how you found my diamond bracelet."

Mrs. Greenstreet said, "This is my home; the big white one, with the bright red shutters." She called to her husband, "Tom! Tom! Come out here, there is someone special I would like you to meet." "Yes dear, what is it?", Mr. Greenstreet said, as he came to the front door. "This is Jake and his wonderful dog, Jil-a-ma-joo." "Hi Jake, how are you doing?", said Mr. Greenstreet "and hello to you, Jil-a-ma-joo," he said, as he patted him on the head.

Mrs. Greensteet told him the whole exciting story about Jake finding her diamond bracelet. Mr. Greenstreet said, "Well, dear, I must say you have had a terrible day today, but thanks to Jake, it turned out to have a very happy ending." "I'm sure proud of you son," he said, as he shook Jake's hand. "A job well done."

She told Mr. Greenstreet about the reward money she wanted to give to Jake for being so honest. "That would be very nice," he said. Mrs. Greenstreet went into the house and came out with an envelope in her hands. She handed it to Jake and said, "This is for you Jake, a check for $100.00." "WOW!" said Jake, "I'm so excited. Thank you very, very much." "Be sure to give it to your Mom as soon as you get home," Mrs. Greenstreet said. "Why don't you write your telephone number on this piece of paper for me, so I can call up your Mom right away." she said. "Here's a bright gold pen for you to use." "O.K." said Jake.

ARF! ARF!

16

"Well, we had better be getting on home, Jil-a-ma-joo. It's getting late and we don't want Mom to start worrying about us. I can't wait to tell Mom and Dad about what happened to us today. They will not believe their ears."

"Besides, it's almost dinner time and I am absolutely starving. How about you, Jilly?" "ARF, ARF," barked Jilly! "I thought so," said Jake.

"Can we have our Chauffeur drive you both home, so you can get home safely?" "Oh no," said Jake. "Thank you anyway. We know a short way home and we'll be there in no time."

Skip to my loo my
JIL-A-MA-JOO

"Anyhow, I'm too excited to sit in a car. I'm going to skip all the way home. Come on, let's go Jilly."

"Goodbye, Mrs. Greenstreet! Goodbye Mr. Greenstreet!"

"Bye, Jake and Jil-a-ma-joo. Thanks again. Come visit us again soon."

Jake started singing, *Skip, skip, skip to my loo, skip, skip, skip to my loo, Skip, skip, skip to my loo ---- Skip to my loo, my JIL-A-MA-JOO!*

I love you, Jilly.

Printed in the United States
by Baker & Taylor Publisher Services